THE ROAD HOME

By **Bernhard Brender**

Neue Auflage 2019
The People I met on the Road Home!

HANNURY Media

It is true. We are people on the move, pilgrims on their way home. If we do not know where we are going, any road will lead us anywhere.

Planning your ways wisely in this life is the only answer.

Going through nine countries on four continents, you are a foreigner and must act accordingly in order to be accepted.

You must be honest and humble, with an open heart and mind, building in stages trusty relationships with the people around you.

The challenge each day is to plan like an adult, but stay humble and honest like a child.

I shall pass through this world but once, any good that I

can do, or any kindness that I can show to any human being, let me not defer nor neglect it, for I shall not pass this way again.

May this short humble compellation of life lessons I've learned on my journey help guide you on your own path home.

Shall peace, happiness, optimism and hope, give you strength and courage to lead you across the bridges of all opportunities in your life, where ever they may take you!

Full of
Sincere
Friendship

밀레니엄 서울힐튼 총지배인 번하드 브랜더의 가슴에 영광스런 훈장이
하나 더 생겼다. 서울시 명예시민으로 선정된 한국의 더 좋은 친구가
자신만큼이나 따뜻한 마음을 지닌 지인들을 초대해 행복한 가든파티를 마련했다.

Bernhard Brender
Special Dedications

First and foremost, to Our Lord Jesus Christ and the blessed Virgin Mary. Their guidance and blessings each day bring us closer to God the Father Almighty.

To my wife, Mutaty Diaz Vera Brender, who gave me two extraordinary daughters Luisa and Alexandra; providing my balanced of Life.

To my family back home in Germany, England+ Indonesia+Korea and USA, for being there in good and challenging times. Father Edmund+Mother Luise, Schwester Maria+Otto, Eugen+Heidi~ Fridolin+Janet, Edmund+ Gabi~ Anton+Angelika+Werner. und Anne.

To all the people who have touched our lives and gave us their love and understanding, from the bottom of my heart, Thank You!~ Dankeschoen~ Terimakasi Banjak~ Kamsahamnida.

TABLE OF CONTENTS

FORWARD

*P*lanning your way wisely in this life is the only answer.
Born between the hills of the black forest in a tiny
village just after the World War II which Germany began.

Going through nine countries on three continents, you are
a foreigner and must act accordingly in order to be accepted.
You must be honest and humble, with an open heart and
mind, building slowly a trust relationship with the people
around you. The challenge each day is to plan like an adult.
But stay humble and honest like a child.

Be flexible, accompanied with a patient attitude. It is the
tool for Rocky hills, We go through in our life.

As the Sun creates your shadow, God created your soul and mind. Nevertheless, in each case. It is you who determine the shape of it.

Shall peace, happiness, optimism and hope do give strength and courage, that lead you to cross the bridges in your life.

Amongst 6.6 billion people on this planet, we only get to meet but a small fraction of them. I'm honored to say that of this small fraction I have met the most amazing people, who have touched my heart, challenged and inspire me.

Grusswort

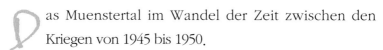as Muenstertal im Wandel der Zeit zwischen den Kriegen von 1945 bis 1950.

Eine unverrueckte Tatsache ist: Auch in der Ferne bleibt man mit dem Geburtsort fest verbunden. Geboren im Spielweg 7 in eine siebenkoepfige katholische Familie unter der Obhut von Mutter Luise und Vater Edmund Brender. Je weiter von der Heimat entfernt, desto staerker werden die Gefuehle von Sehnsucht und Verlangen seinem Geburtsort mit Leib und Seele verbunden zu sein.

Getragen durch den Herzenswunsch, dadurch Einsamkeit und allein sein zu entfliehen. Wenn man eine Kindheit voller Waerme. Liebe und Geborgenheit im Muenstertal erleben durfte, kann man auch die oftmals in der weiten Welt vorherschende Kaelte und Verlorenheit besser ertragen.

Seit 1963 auf vier Kontinenten in einer neuen Umgebung zuhause, dabei in 10 Laendern vorueber gehend sesshaft geworden um zu arbeiten und das taegliche Brot zu verdienen.

Trotz abenteuerlichen Reisen, unvergesslicher Erlebnisse und der Freude, dabei auch die engliche Sprache erlernen zu koennen.

Um weltweit verstanden zu sein. Er giebt sich die Chance andere Kulturen kennen zu lernen und respectiert zu werden. Es blieb und bleibt die starke Verbindung zur Heimat und die Wurzeln zum Muenstertal im Herzen erhalten.

Soll doch der Wander-Rucksack gefuellt sein mit globalem Wissen, festem Glauben und toleranter Lebenseinstellung als gesunde Nahrung zum Ueberleben des immer wieder herausfordenden Alltages in der Ferne. Verbunden mit der Hoffnung, dabei genug stille Reserven eingepackt zu haben. um die Sehnsucht nach Geborgenheit in meiner geliebten Heimat Muenstertal auf Ewigkeit im Herzen zu tragen. Ich wuensche Dir. lieber Freund Manfred und deiner lieben Frau Sieglinde weiterhin alles erdenklich Gute und Kraft,das geliebte Muenstertal auch weiterhin mit deiner Arbeit zu bereichern auch von Staufen aus.

My Life, My Family Story

$\mathcal{I}$ had no say in selecting the country and culture in which I was to be born, the choice of parents~ home and religion, all this was simply decided for me. Right after the end of World War II in 1945 which Germany began and lost. I was born into a time of no hope~ moral~ stability and leadership. There was only distraction~ hate and misery.

My Motherland was stricken by an evil ego-driven dictator called Adolf Hitler/SS. If it would not have been for the

Marshal Plan enforced by U.S. President Roosevelt, our hope for a future was slim.

For this I am and will always be grateful to the Americans calling them my Heroes.

As a token of Appreciation for the Marshal Plan I gave my own Blood through my daughters to USA. The eldest Luisa married Shane an American who live in West Virginia-and Alexandra married Michael Ferullo as well an American live in Huston Texas.

This Photo is the proof of my honest contribution to America. A small payback for the Marchal Plan.

Merry Christmas
The Brenders
2017 - 2018

What brought my parents together was out of the ordinary. My mother Luise was born into a wine growing Familie into the Gasthaus Sonne in Soelden close to Freiburg/Breisgau in Sued Baden. She cooked for various guests that passed through her tiny village in Germany. My father Edmund was one of them.

He was born into a brush making Factory im Obermuenstertal, 40 kilometers from Soelden. On his way to do business in Freiburg Father Edmund would often stop by my mother's place for a hearty meal. Needless to say, he started to admire my mother working in the Kitchen. Then after months of eating Luise's delicious Food my Father ask Luise out one Night to see a Movie in Freiburg.

My Mother for the first time out of her hot kitchen to go to see a Movie in Freiburg was a big deal. When they arrived in Freiburg in front of the theater my Mother suddenly asks Edmund, "Why spend money for a movie? Let's just walk and enjoy the fresh Air" and so they did. That night Edmund was able to discover Luise's inner human values such as her deep faith as a Catholic and saving Money.

Since Mother Luisa cooked well my Father Edmund was convinced never to be hungry again He ask Luise's Father, for her hand in Marry her and he did. That is how it all started and brought them together for life. The fruits of their

Marriage brought them 6 healthy Boys and one Sister all still alive today.

Together, Mother Luise and Father Edmund created a cozy home for us. 6 Brothers and one Sister, built on faith, unconditional love, and Care for one another.

First born our brother Eugen July 09 1938. He was our Guardien Angel. with his responsibility of taking care of all his siblings, which in itself had many sacrifices. He went on to marry the charming Heidi, born and raised in Munich. Next in line was Fridolin born in June, 03 1940 who went on to become a respected Pastry Chef in London. He married Janet and they have two beautiful daughters, Jacqueline married to Nick and Julia to Garret having Taylor as their Son. Edmund was born 1944, he married a talented Hairdresser Gabi. They have Sascha and Mark both certified Steinmetz Stone Masters. Having their own Business.

Fourth was me, nicknamed "Bollili" or "BB". I married Mutaty Diaz Vera from Bali/Lombog, born in Timor Kupang, Indonesia. Together we have two daughters, Luisa and Alexandra. The only Lady amongst 6 brothers was Maria married Otto. The next brother Anton, Evi, daughter Sabine and Angelika. The last of the Brender was Werner born Sep

9th 1956. He is a Steinmetz Master and decorated with the Golden Meisster brief. He has two children, Johanna and Phillip and Is together with Anne.

With such a large family it is essential to have faith and love to keeping us together. That is why Mother Mary, the Mother of Jesus, is always at the center of our lives. With so many brothers and only one sister Maria, we learned at an early stage, to share Food+Cloth+Toy's and pray together. Especially right after the World War II, We all are equipped with such Inner values ready to conquer the real cold World. Sharing cloth from the older brothers was one way to safe Money a smart Mother's Plain.

On the Road from my tiny village Obermuenstertal in Schwarzwald (Black Forest) has since brought me from Germany to Switzerland, England, Philippines, Indonesia, Thailand, Kenya, Hong Kong and South Korea. Throughout my journey I've met such extraordinary people who have touched my heart and mind.

The key Message I got from Anselm Gruen is "Die hohe Kunst des Alterwerdens. Getting older is no big Deal, but to manage your Age is the big deal. Therefore invest your time do not waste it!

Balance of Life

Y ou can either agree or disagree that balance stops and
starts between our ears. The mind and mouth, with
two moving lips, play an important role in whether we keep
or lose our balance.

1. Lately, I see and hear more people struggling with their
balance than ever before. Has the world changed? Is the
world spinning faster than it has for the last 4.6 billion years?
Does the Climate Change is changing us too. In fact our we
need Mother Nature because Nature has its own way and we
have to adjust and respect no choice.

Our brains, like a silver roulette wheel, are so easily

influenced by the outside world. After receiving opinions from readers about my past articles, I get the ugly impression of bodies with hands reaching out in all directions for help losing their Balance of Life.

One in particular I remember is a Thai lady calling me after she read an article of mine relating to religion. She said, "Thank you for showing me the Road Home. Another time a man called to vent his anger, after reading another article, "Peace is flowing like a River." He told me, "You must be joking! There is no peace in this world, not even in my own family. Whoever you are, you must be living in a cave, so just come out of it. Tell me, where is the river of peace flowing that you claim to have seen?"

I spent about 10 minutes with him on the phone, sharing my experiences from last July in Lourdes, France. One hundred and twenty-five years ago, the mother of Jesus appeared to the poor miller's daughter, Bernadette Soubiros (St. Bernadette) eighteen times asking her to pray the rosary. Up until now sixty-five healing miracles have occurred there ever since, and it is best known as the "Miracle of Lourdes."

He asked many questions, and I could tell he was at the

edge of his patience, ready to eat me alive through the phone. He hung up the phone suddenly, leaving no name or phone number.

A few months later, a letter came to my office saying, "My life is back to normal. I have found my inner peace and balance. Prayers healed my wounds." This was for me a great moment of joy, though I knew nothing about him. I sincerely hope today that my strange friend reads this and takes the credit for today's title "Balance" helping others to find their balance of Life as well.

On Thursday the 28th of May, 1992 at 07:34 am. a German friend here in Seoul called me up just to tell me that I had spoiled his breakfast. He had ordered his regular breakfast through room service: two fried eggs, two slices of bacon, sausages, toast, coffee, and porridge. In addition to that, with his health in mind of course, he also got fruit yoghurt and a fresh banana.

While he was waiting he opened as usual his morning paper, The Korea Times. He became stuck on page, where my name was next to the article titled, "Eating Habits and Trends" in the Thought of the Times section. Shall I cancel my breakfast? No, I will call Brender instead and tell him to mind his own business. But instead he complimented me on the article that I wrote, "Bernhard, can you tell me how much fat is too much? How many cigarettes and cups of coffee are reasonable? How much should I exercise?"

The answer to his questions was easy, "The less fat, the better, and start exercising, but ask the health club manager to guide you.

"Wait a moment, I hear the doorbell ring. I think it's the room service." Sure enough it was the room service knocking at his hotel room door. I could almost smell the fried eggs and bacon through the phone.

"Go and eat your breakfast", I said.

"Just another question," he replied. "Tell me, how many calories are in two fried eggs and two strips of bacon?"

"Do you really want to know that now? Go and eat your breakfast."

"Yes, but tell me first, then I will eat my breakfast."

"Okay, two fried eggs have 230 calories, and the two strips of bacon, 85 calories." Then I told him, "You must run six minutes or swim 10 minutes or bicycle 13 minutes, or walk 22 minutes or aerobic dance 13 minutes to burn them off. As you can see, much more exercise is needed." My German friend became so silent that I asked, "Are you still there?"

Then he kept on talking, "What is fitness exactly?"

I told him, your breakfast is getting cold, but this is a good question. I remembered Dr. Robert Butler's smart remark, "If exercising could be packed into a pill, it would be the single most widely prescribed and beneficial medicine in the world."

Suddenly he asked, "How many calories do you burn while you are talking?"

I told him, "A liar burns up to 1000 calories per minute." We both started laughing our heads off. Miraculously, he told me after laughing that he felt much better.

I wonder how many calories we actually do burn during a minute of laughter. My grandmother used to say that laughter was healthy. This is actually very true. It has been proven that laughter releases endorphins, a natural mood enhancer, and increases circulation. The Moral of the story, laughter is medicine!

Fitness is different for different people, you must agree. Some people think of it as someone jumping up and down. Others think of a grunting muscular man pumping iron. For me, fitness is expressed in the simplest manner, its the "dynamic state of mind and body" far away from hours of television viewing, weak muscles, low esteem, easy fatigue, poor body shape, backaches, and no prayers.

Frankly our muscles, heart, and lungs, are wonderful pieces of machinery. Let us include them in our daily lives because life is a gift to be treasured. Every time we act, we should think of our health.
Our bodies are the ultimate vessel of life.

A most rewarding instance of sharing experiences with people came again through the phone on Saturday 27th February 1993 at 11:35 am. A Korean lady called me and said, "The article you wrote, 'Life is a Gift', helped me to find my balance back, which was destroyed years ago by my own mother."

We are constantly in a balancing act. We have to balance our job and private lives. Be fair to all parties concerned. Equally balance your time between guests, the boss, your children, your friends and peers.

Avoid wasting; try instead to invest valuable time equally between them. Where are you investing your time? We should all be mastered by the two bodily bosses, the mind and the heart. Don't starve, but eat a balanced meal with less fat like Tajana said.

I met June 22nd Tatjana and Rolf Widmer from Switzerland during the June 22/23 2019 WFF Universe Korea Contest.

Tatjana told me that she won just recently the European Contest 2019 and here at the GHS she got the Ms. Universe Title in her Category Body Building. She said focusing on what you eat and drink, balanced with consistence Body exercise is the secret of the Balance Body of Mind.

The Road FC at the Paradise Miss Kim and Miss Lee guided me through the Master Champion Ship without Nose

bleeding, Thanks God for that.

A most rewarding instance of sharing experiences with people came again through the phone on Saturday 27th February 1993 at 11:35 am. A Korean lady called me and said, "The article you wrote, 'Life is a Gift', helped me to find my balance back, which was destroyed years ago by my own mother."

We are constantly in a balancing act. We have to balance our job and private lives. Be fair to all parties concerned. Equally balance your time between guests, the boss, your children, your friends and peers.

Avoid wasting; try instead to invest valuable time equally between them. Where are you investing your time? We should all be mastered by the two bodily bosses, the mind and the heart. Don't starve, but eat a balanced meal with less fat. Increase the amount of time you devote to exercise. Avoid waiting for tomorrow because it might never come. Love first to be loved, and respect first to be respected. Rush down the freeway of health and happiness. Balanced with the wisdom of today's message, supported by daily prayers, and strive for the sure road home.

Life is a Gift

*A*re we taking life for granted in our days? Is life meaningless in the real sense, or did we lose the connection between the mind and heart, and our actions? Why do many people have to get killed everyday? The United States government is currently undergoing the fight between good and evil because of abortion. People do not love God anymore. Is this true? Regardless of our beliefs and principles, do we have the right to do anything we feel like doing? Is it a matter of kill or be killed, even with unborn infants?

Yes, for sure we have lost the real value of life, otherwise why do so many people decide to remove unborn infants out from their mothers' womb, and throw them out.

Where is our respect and value for life? Our pleasure and desires have taken over and they promote convenience as happiness.

One is innocent until proven guilty, preaches the western world. Here, in Korea, they say that the moment he or she caught in the act, he or she is guilty. How can we trust each other, when evil is ever present in our attitudes and sense of self-justified morality?

Friends keep on asking me, "Why me? Why do I get so sick, and nobody can help me, am I going to die? Oh, God has abandoned me. God is not fair. I have not done anything wrong!"

I have a precise answer to that: God has not abandoned us, we have abandoned Him. We do not have patience with other people anymore, and we are quick to quarrel, quick to get angry without genuine reason. Why? Has the respect for one another gone out of the world?

Often I am asked if God has been present in Auswitsch during the most devastating Crimes against 6 Million Jewish

People? I can only say God was present and suffered at the same time because he gave freedom to choose between Evil and Good. To put my guild German brain to peace, I hope with the Grace of God he accepted those Merthyers into Heaven.

What happened to our leadership abilities? Leading by example is the most powerful management style in our modern business-minded world. A boss who is bossy is not a leader at all. A boss who points and tells you "Go " is not a leader; a leader is someone who says "Let's Go" and does it. Actions speak louder than words.

Does one have to be born to be a leader? Who among the leaders we have known from the past and present believes that "LIFE IS A GIFT."

Here are some obvious examples of good and bad leaders, The Evil Adolf Hitler versus the holy, Mother Theresa.

Jesus gave His life for us as a "GIFT" and he sacrifice of His blood on the cross to set us "FREE" from sins and give us eternal life. The only challenge is that one has to believe in him and have faith.

Therefore each of us has a difficult task to bring joy to others. No reason is good enough to exclude others from being a part of our lives. If we exclude them we only become poorer and crippled in an ocean of ignorance, hatred and destruction in the world today. This message comes as a healing balm to a wound.

We need leaders who value human life over all other things. If a leader is to lead a nation to be better human beings, to improve their quality of life.

We can do something daily for peace. We can love each other, be more courteous, more thoughtful. We strengthen our prayers—the ultimate weapon for peace.

Finally, a poem that is tailor made for our subject, "Life is a gift." This might be the answer that we are searching for.

LIFE IS A GIFT

I will lend you for a little time, a child of mine, God said.

For you to love while he lives, and mourn when he is dead.

It may be six or seven years, or twenty-two or three.

But will you, till I call him back, take care of him for me?

He'll bring his charms to gladden you, and shall his stay be brief.

You'll have his lovely memories as solace of your grief. I cannot

promise he will stay, since all from earth return.

Yet there are lessons taught down here. I want this child to learn.

I've looked the wide world over in my search for teachers true.

And from the throngs that crowd life's lanes, I have selected you.

Now will you give him all your love, nor think the labor vain. Nor

hate me when I come to call, to take him back again?

I fancied that I hear them say, "Dear Lord Thy will be done. For

all the joy thy child shall bring, the risk grief we run."

We'll shelter him with tenderness, we'll love him while we may;

and for the happiness we've known; will ever grateful stay.

Nevertheless, shall the angels call for him much sooner than we

planned.

We'll be brave for the bitter grief that comes, and try to

understand.

This poem has helped many people, as I hope it will help us too. Every once in a while we have to re-evaluate our basic principles, just like taking a hot bath from time to time (since Korea has the best saunas in the world).

Just take a moment and relax giving your Body a Break.

Respect the little things, because the little things mean a lot. Love first to receive love, respect first to be respected.

Rush down the freeway of health and happiness, balanced with wisdom, love and care for each other.

The best choice we have is to beat the devil, with the help from God. Satan knows that the spirit is strong but the flesh is weak.

Korean-German Goethe Story

Prof. {em} Dr. Chashik Shin {berno} German department Dankook University.

He created a noble GOETHE STORY in Briefmarken Philatelie Stamps. The best in the global market and you have to order and read it.

His e-mail is bernoshin@hanmail.net

Mobile 82-10-3385-3167

Time Management
in a Time of Crisis

I was very impressed with the answer Kim Ki-Hoon gave the press at the 1992 Winter Olympics in Albertville, France. He had won Korea's first-ever gold medal at any Winter Olympics.

In his polite, modest and humble way he said, "I trained hard and did my best and I won the gold. I am very happy." His skills, endurance and timing, has paid off with a gold medal.

He did not say, "I knew I would win the gold because I am the best."

Time Management is the most popular topic of our day.

Managing time simply means saving time. One cannot buy nor borrow time. Nevertheless, you and I can save our time and the time of others.

There are people amongst us who waste food, beverages, health, money and equipment. However, the biggest crime is wasting valuable time. A watch only tells you time, moves where you want, and keeps on ticking.

Can I measure, control and plan time, my own and that of others? If sales persons come late for an appointment, they usually blame the traffic or their watches. The problem is not the traffic or the watch.

The problem is poor time management skills. Let us measure some basic time elements from Mother Nature. A normal baby in a mother's womb spends nine months there. The average life span of Korean woman is seventy-two years. For the average Korean male it is sixty-nine years. Why do women live longer? Is it because men work, smoke and drink more than women?

Let us observe the season's timing:

Winter:	December	—	February
Spring:	March	—	May
Summer:	June	—	August
Autumn:	September	—	November

Which season is the most important? Which one suits you best? Obviously, every season is as important as every part of your body is. The ears, arms, legs, stomach, eyes, mouth, nose, hands and mind.

If one body part is out of order, you are out of order.

The real meaning of SUPEX (Super Excellence) is simply to develop a super mind and spirit, super health, eyes, ears, hands, attitude and care. If we are super, our job becomes automatically superb. That is what super excellence (SUPEX) is all about. Short cuts do not pay off, and therefore in the end, do not save time. Cutting policies and procedures does not pay off. They cost you more time in retraining and rebuilding. The solution is no short cut please.

Our daily job performance and job tasks require a super mind. The employees and workers must have the opportunity to develop a truly independent mind with the job objective at hand. In a hotel it is every employee's responsibility to ensure that the guest has a hospitable, enjoyable stay. A hotel only reaches the five-star level of service when each employee has a super attitude then we reach Gold.

What are Time Management skills exactly? From whom can we learn them? We all have twenty-four hours available everyday. Some people work at night and sleep during the day. Some working mothers have two jobs and don't have time for sleep at all. Nine hours of hard productive work should be enough. Seven hours of sleep will give our body time to build the necessary energy. If you work hard during the daytime, you will be tired at night. If I do not allow your body to sleep, soon the body will go on striking physically and mentally. There is still eight hours for us to either waste or to invest wisely in education, exercise, sports, relaxation, or for the spirit of the family.

Some people do not realize the value of time. With that they become apart of a circle of destruction. The truth is they do not even notice it. They are losers, trouble makers, and they have less than five hours sleep. They are moody, weak, and cannot mange time. They talk too much and fear advances. They become professional losers. I call them walking time bombs. They have left the circle of improvement and are stuck in their own dire routine trying to just stay afloat.

Because of this they don't have time and forget to search for knowledge, to go for quality instead of quantity. They forget to try positive thinking be innovative and creative. Let's bring them back to the circle of improvement that belongs to the winners. They think positively and help to build team spirit. They give their best everyday for nine hours. They settle for the best; they go for the gold!

What are the four major communication channels within companies, hotels, government offices, etc.?

1. What can I expect from my employees?

2. What does my superior expect from me?
3. What do my subordinates expect from me?
4. What do I expect from my subordinates?

The result shows clearly that your expectations are the same as your Employees,

Coaching and counseling +Open mind+ a super mind+ Fair pay

Objective communication* Share goals and knowledge Recognition

Respect+Cooperation+Positive thinking+Trust+ Listening

Let us spend enough time training to improve our skills with time management. Let us look at some of our time related expectations. How soon do we expect an e-mail to reach us, of course at once.

A chef boils eggs for four minutes. He cannot blame the egg when it is under or over cooked. Use an egg timer. A room maid has to makeup fourteen rooms per day and each room takes thirty-five minutes for a Total of 490minutes or eight hours.

Eating Habits and Trends

While eating, cooking, and serving food and beverages for the last thirty-eight years in nine countries and three continents, I have encountered the most haunting question, "What shall I eat? " People with little food in their hands and stomachs show the extreme contrast of having too much food available, not knowing what to eat, and being afraid of becoming too fat.

Lots of people are overweight or underweight with no exercise or too much of it. Too many people lack balance, shape, time and motivation. Tell me what you eat, and I'll simply tell you who you are. Either willingly or unwillingly, many eat unhealthy food and get sick; this is the law of nature. When people are smart to choose healthy food, they stay healthy.

In order to keep fit, you must exercise to burn your calories and to circulate your blood; there is no way around it. In this manner, you will be moving in the right direction.

What a farmer does not know, he won't eat. Why do children always settle for ice-cream and sweets? Is it because the body wants or needs it? We know children do not like vegetables, but they willingly go with their parents into MacDonald's restaurant. Often, the father's end up with the big Mac (this of which I am guilty), but has too many calories.

Are we slaves of the media and TV campaigns? Why does a German prefer sausages, mustard and beer, the Japanese their sushi and sashimi, the English with their steak with an English pint, and finally the Koreans their delicious kalbi and kimchi with soju? Traditions are very strong in any society, especially when it comes to food. Food is an integral part of any culture.

Secrets to live long and healthy.

Let's do it and crack the nutshell go into the healthy eating Habit. Here are some guidelines:

Exercise regularly+Eat less+Thinks positively and be stress free+Stop smoking now+Eat fresh Food and reduce salt intake. Just do it.

- Garlic is healthy. It strengthens your artery walls and prevents plaque build up in the blood stream. Keep on eating, and don't worry about the after effects. Some eundan, silver peppermint pills will eliminate the aroma.
- Drink ginseng tea or tonic supplements, it's good for blood circulation
- Eat one kiwi fruit a day and eat a fresh apple a day to keep the Doctor away
- Take a glass of warm Water each morning to an empty Stomach it will be good for your health.
- Eat balanced meals with fresh fish and vegetables, eat less red meat.
- Go for pigeon that has no cholesterol and is full of nutritious value.
- Use fresh products available at the open market.

- High fiber, whole grains, unbleached products
- Fresh herbs and spices
- Use oil of olives, soybeans, peanuts and sesame
- Limit your use of salted butter, cream and dairy products (low-fat)

  Prepare everything fresh. Preservatives are not your friend.

  Aim for tasty foods with a natural aroma
- Dry beans and seaweed
- Important recommendations: making good use of omega-3 fatty acids (salmon, tuna, cod, trout and herring)
- Vegetables
- Pasta (in moderation)
- Brown rice
- Use good low fat protein sources
- Poultry without skin: the pigeon is the best meal
- Using cooking methods to reduce fat
- Grilling, steaming, poaching, broiling, baking, microwave, etc.
- All the above guidelines are online with and accepted by

Do's
- The US recommended Daily Allowance
- The American Heart Association

- The World Health Organization
- The American Cancer Society
- The US Dietary Goals

DON'TS:

- Canned food if possible
- Frozen meats
- Preserved smoked food
- Skin of poultry
- Processed Cheeses
- Salted Butter
- Bleached Sugar
- Preservatives
- MSG (Monosodium Glutamate)
- Heavy sauces

If all of the above health experts give you their blessings, it simply means that you are on the right track.

We know the life span of women in Korea is 72, and men's is 68.

Both have their Do and Don't to live longer and more healthy.

With this new eating philosophy, you're on your way to a long way to a healthier and more successful life.

Maria Apparition

The phone rang exactly at 5:45 AM. on Saturday 8th January, 1994. At 6:00 AM. sharp, our driver S.P. Jeon drove us safely to the bus terminal. An express bus, drove by Mr. Hahn, brought my wife and two young daughters safely to Naju; it is in the Cholla-Namdo Province that is four hours away from Seoul by car.

There, we visited Julia Kim and we saw proof of the statue of our Blessed Mother who shed tears of blood for 700 days, beginning from 1985. Julia told us to pray, pray, pray!

In Naju, South Korea, a statue of the Virgin Mary shed its first tears of blood. This was a message urging people to choose a righteous way of life and return to God and repent. However, most people are too busy with their own daily lives. They make their own rules as they go.

"Now, I want to plead with you with my last Tears of Blood. Now, hurry up and come, all the children in the world!"

TEL: 82-61-334-5003
Web: www.najumary.or.kr
Facebook: https: www.youtube.com/najumary
Address: The Chapel of the Blessed Mother of Naju 12, Najucheon 2 gil,
Naju City, Jeonnam, 58258, South Korea

Avoiding Risks is Pretty Risky

In September 1992, at the Central Plaza Hotel and Convention Centre in Bangkok, right after my lecture on "Time Management in Times of Crisis," a middle-aged overweight man ran after me and squeezed my arm. With watery eyes and a soft voice, he told me, "Your lecture comes too late, at least for me, I lost everything, and I am finished." His swollen face and nervous eyes made me guilty and worried I asked him, "Why and how did you loose everything? " Almost in a whisper he replied, "I always avoided taking risks in my life, I went along with the crowd, never hurting or cheating anybody. I always helped and listened to other people."

My heart became soft, ears wide open and we went together for a drink. A cold beer at the right time does miracles. It unleashed the tongue of my amputated friend and his heart breaking story came out slowly into the open air. Since then, my personal policy has been to share valuable experience with others, so keep on reading···.

They write many valuable books on risk taking. My favorite books are those by Gene Calvert, in it many patterns parallel with my personal experience.

In a crazy world spiced daily with uncertainly, companies are putting pressure on managers to perform. Maybe you are one of them who have to raise and stimulate revenue and profit, elevate staff morale and respond to competitive threats.

"Take risks everyday. Nothing else will do! " Let me tell you, even if you are on the right track, you get ran over if you just sit there and wait. In moving forward, you have to take risks. Remember, taking risks is the only way to innovate, generate exceptional profits, and to reach your highest aspirations. Whether you work for an old, new, small, big or high profit organization, the principle is still the same. The title you have with the company's fine reputation cannot secure and make your name and future. You must build it yourself.

No risk in itself is risky. Successful managers take many medium-sized risks. They are neither conservative nor fool hardy. This shows that personal bases and frames of references can distort your view of the potential gains or losses of a risky decision. Intuition can be a valuable partner in decision making.

My experiences with Intercontinental, Sheraton, Hilton Hotels, over the last 46 years, show how intuition and risks are essential in surviving in the business world today. Smart managers spread the danger of the risk around by building consensus.

Most of the colleagues I have met fear taking risks.

Obviously, walking on a tight-rope crossing the management high wire, is a skill everybody can and should learn. Just develop a sense of balance, and maintain a reliable safety net. Then you will learn how to perceive the length and condition of the wire.

Whether you prefer to take or avoid risks, the truth is:

Risks are persuasive. They are a part of every decision you

make or avoid.

*Risks are inevitable. Avoiding one risk merely creates another the risk of not risking.

*Risks have costs that may range from a slap on the wrist to organization to bankruptcy.

There realities lurk behind every decision you make, whether it is setting priorities, cutting costs, allocating funds, developing products, or delegating tasks. How well you anticipate, assess and deal with these challenges, determine how well the organization does and how far you go in your career.

Let us now look at some possible strategies: Avoid danger:

First you can choose not to risk. Sometimes, this is a wise course but remember that "not risking is also a risk." Have an argument ready in the event someone tries to pin the blame on you, you can abandon a risk anytime. Deals are like taxis on the road. There is always another one coming. The next deal might be better than the one you walked away from.

• Limit danger:

This is very appropriate to the Korean business world. You

can limit danger by negotiating longer deadlines, obtaining better information, and adjusting your decisions. You can also employ experts to help defuse dangers. Experts, however, rarely provide a single correct solution to your problem, so. Don't hand your fate over to them.

• Share the danger:

You can share danger too. Create alliances, partnerships, or join ventures. Pooling intellectual and financial resources, limits the amount of loss suffered by anyone party and increases the group's willingness to pursue hazardous ventures. Executives here in Korea try to generate as much as harmony for the risks they take. The board of directors, the first level of risk taking.

Partners, must be involved early on.

• Growth in danger zone:

Take calculated, but not wildly reckless risks. That would endanger the company or your career needlessly. Aim instead for "affordable" risks that you might otherwise shy away from.

• The reward of risking:

Why should you brave the risk high wire when you can

stroll safely on the ground? The lesson in larger risk produces greater profits, which fuel growth and provide funds to pay off Debts and finance other profitable risks.

When the status quo has no future and predictions will not hold true, risk oriented manager's find opportunities and rewards by taking voluntary risks more often. We must unleash leadership ability. Excellence and willingness to share, when we think globally and perform to native conditions, there is a proof that Intentional risk-takers earn.

Great respect, recognition, pride and confidence.

The average risk-taker manager, in contrast, rarely turns career dreams into reality. Executives who walk the management high wire get maximum self-fulfillment from their careers. On closing note you must agree: one of the best reasons to take risks is to find out just.

How good you really are!

Learn from failure and enjoy the valuable gifts of insight and information. You learn to risk by doing it, just do it, and you will stay alive. You will not reach the end of the rope so quickly like the Business friend I made in Bangkok in 1992.

By the way, his eyes are dry, he weighs less and he is back on his feet, taking more calculated risks. His glass is always half full, instead of half empty. He is a newborn optimist.

Finally something else on a personal note to relate to business and risk. In spirit and respect to all religions on earth leading to God, you must agree that without any doubt, Satan is by far, the most busy and successful businessman in the world today, harvesting souls into his kingdom of hell, forever disconnected with the living God in Heaven.

Now, would you honestly want to throw your life away and to go to hell, if there is even a 1% chance that God exists?

Seek Him and you will find Him. Trust me!

Peace is flowing like a River

D o Lourdes and the name of Bernadette mean anything to you? Although the event is more than 135 years old, it is still freshly flowing like a river today. It is a sign of hope, love and peace to humankind.

My promise to my daughters Luisa and Alexandra, and wife Taty, were completed on June 27~30, 1993. During that time, we spent four days in Lourdes, France. No words can describe the expressions and positive attitudes of 20,000 pilgrims daily from around the world in sick and in health conditions. Muslim, Buddhist, Hindu, Atheists, Protestants and Catholics are astonished of the event that is so powerful, complete, true and very simple.

In silence, they admired such grace from God, and move willingly into a newborn approach of life. That many roads lead to heaven is almost true, but to follow the road that Jesus gave us cannot be wrong. Now his mother visits us and moves lasting doubts of our troubles minds and hearts.

The visit from heaven, in a small town in the Pyrenees of France called Lourdes, is her destiny to the world. This began on February 11th, 1858 with the 1st apparition of the "Immaculate Conception" to Bernadette Soubirous. From then onwards, millions of pilgrims from every part of the world would come to pray before the grotto where the apparitions took place. So, Lourdes becomes a special place for the Christians, and experience of faith and of the Gospel. It gives hope of healing for the sick, a source of strength for every afflicted heart, a reason to live, and for many it is a push to open the Bible. Believers are reinforced to weekly fasting, praying the rosary, and the reconciliation with the living God.

Since 1858, doctors have examined about 6,000 miracle-cases of cures. Of these, the competent ecclesiastical authorities have declared sixty-four miracles. An important thing to note is that many cures have been considered medically inexplicable by the International Medical Committee in Paris.

Who was Bernadette? She was the daughter of a miller reduced to poverty, who was humbled, young and religious. A girl who is consciously and generously spent her short life in suffering. Bernadette was privileged to have eighteen apparitions from 11th February until 16th July 1858. Think for a moment that she spoke to the mother of Jesus, and saw Holy Mother of God with her own eyes; can you understand and grasp this phenomenon? I don't think so.

February 11th, 1858 was the first Thursday in Lent. A mist surrounded Lourdes but there was no rain. It was about eleven in the morning and in the Soubirous family home at Cachot it was cold and there was no more firewood. Antoinette and Jeanne Abadie accompanied Bernadette to a thicket at Massabielle to gather sticks to heat their home.

When they got as far as the Savy mill, instead of going to the wood, they followed the mill race till it brought them before the grotto.

As Bernadette took off her stockings to cross the stream, the 1st apparition occurred. "I saw a lady dressed in white. She wore a white dress and a white veil with a blue waist band and a yellow rose on each of her feet. Her rosary was yellow too. The lady took the rosary from her arm and made a sign of the Cross. I wanted and managed to do also. I got down on my knees and began to recite the Rosary with the beautiful Lady. The Lady moved the rosary beads between her fingers without moving her lips. When it was over, she made a sign for me to come near, but I didn't dear to⋯ then suddenly, she disappeared⋯."

The 9th apparitions occurred on 25th February 1858. this apparition took place around five o'clock in the morning. Bernadette and Lucille, Bernadette's aunt and some three hundred other people were present. It had been rained all night and was so cold. Nonetheless, the grotto was literally thronged with people. The invitation to penance gave by Bernadette the previous day was extended and taken a step further. Repentance! Repentance! Repentance! Pray to God for sinners! This is the ninth apparitions that explain the origin of the spring water, still flowing like a river today in Lourdes.

These are Bernadette's words: "The vision told me to go and drink from the spring. Since I could not see it, I went to drink from the river. She told me it was not there. She pointed under the rock, and I was to drink from there. I went there and found only a little blackish water. I put my hand into it but was unable to take any. Then I dug with my hands and so was able to take some. Three times I threw the water away since it was dirty. Then the fourth time, I managed to drink."

In context of the message of Lourdes, the water principally is a sign and invitation to spiritual purification. This was essentially what our Lady wanted. It is not some magic liquid with special healing properties. God sometimes uses the water as a visible sign for some extra ordinary cures for the purposes of showing in a concrete way that He is present in this blessed place, nothing more.

The pilgrim who has come to Lourdes is invited through the sign of the water to renew his Baptismal promises. We are invited to reconciliation with God and with our fellow human being. Confession is nothing other than a bath that purifies the spirit. Go to the fountain to drink and to wash yourselves. Bernadette repeated these gestures often both during and after the apparition but she gave to it the meaning intended by the Immaculate Virgin Mary. A desire to reinvigorate one's faith, affect the message of Lourdes. It is the truth to Mary's initiative.

The 16th apparitions was on 25th March 1858, the Feast of the Annunciation. Some people indulged in the secret hope that something extraordinary would happen, and it did! For her part, Bernadette began to feel again that "irresistible force" and went to the grotto at five o'clock in the morning with her parents. They thought they might be alone, but no, in the half-lighted they say moving shadows Commissar Jacomet, the little seer's implacable observer was there too at the grotto.

Three times, Bernadette asked the apparition who she was. Finally, the answer came Bernadette said, "She went on smiling, so I dared ask her again. This time, however she raised her eyes to heaven and joined her hands about her breast. She said that she was THE IMMACULATE CONCEPTION. These are the last words she addressed to me. Her eyes were blue."

Bernadette died on 16th April 1879 at the age of thirty five. A bronze and crystal casket in which they preserve the body of Bernadette can be seen today at the Convent of St. Gildard at Nevers in France, where Bernadette entered to become a nun in 1866. Bernadette's whole life, her whole mission and message on a piece of paper written:

TO OBEY IS TO LOVE- TO TOLERATE FOR CHRIST IS JOY- TO LOVE SINCERELY IS TO GIVE EVERYTHING, EVEN GRIEF!

Today 161 years later, "THE IMMACULATE CONCEPTION," our Virgin Mary, the mother of Jesus Our Lord, still shows us the way in many places in order to draw us back to reconcile with God.

Six children still see her everyday in Medugorje in Yugoslavia, since June 1981. Here in Korea, only a few hours away from Seoul in Naju, a statue belonging to Ms. Julia Kim shed tears of blood since June 1985 for 700 days like mention above.

Since November 1992, the statue has released perfumed oil to this day.

Are Lourdes+Medujgorje+Naju really sign of times leading to Peace? Find out by yourself if you have time before it is to late.

Marian Apparitions

M any readers are anxious to hear the urgent news from above, I am delighted to share it with you all.

"The Warning," published a little while ago, received a tremendous response, especially from non Christians.

We must be very selective these days on what we hear, see and read. Is the information on TV, in the radio, in magazines and newspapers is it helpful, or harmful to us?

The Miraculous Medal: Paris 1830.

In the year of 1980 marked the 150th anniversary of the first modern apparitions of the Blessed Virgin Mary. On 18th of July, 1830 (to St. Catherine Labourne, then was a young novice from the Sister of Charity, St. the Paul in Paris), our lady spoke these telling words: "The times are very evil, they will plunge the whole world into every kind of trouble."

In that instance, she opened to Catherine and to us the long corridor of modern history, where in so many calamities event have stricken our globe. She clearly took us back to her son Jesus, away from the darkness. Just as she led Catherine from her sleep to the chapel, she was also calling us into the new life in the Lord.

Later she appeared to Catherine to present her with the image that we are familiar with on the miraculous medal. On its force, she stands aside the earth in domination; Satan himself is beneath her hill, while her hands stream light upon the world. She said the rays represent graces given by her intercession to those who have asked for them. Around the oval perimeter of the image, we can read the words, "Oh Mary, conceived without sin, prays for us who have recourse to you."

This prayer signifies her victory over evil, since the Immaculate Conception is a total conquest of sin in a human heart. She leads us into the same victory by her example, and helps us by her prayers to attain it.

In La Salette southern of France, she appeared to two ordinary children, and not particularly religious either. They were herding their cattle when she revealed herself in a glowing vision, as a sorrowful queen. It was the feast of Our Lady's of Sorrow, on 19th September, during that period.

She was weeping, as she moaned to them over the sins of her 'children', complaining that she could "no longer hold back the arms of my son."

Dressed in royal fashioned, the adorned her robes with the instruments of the passion, embroidered on her garments in the light. In correspondence with her prophecies, great potato famine and wheat blight struck Western Europe, and then a convulsive sickness afflicted little children, who died in their mother's arms. In this visitation, her words again clearly assert that people's sins bring them such misfortunes. Farther, she demands repentance! People must obey GOD and His commandments, or punishment will descend upon them.

The year 1854, Pius IX defined the dogma of the Immaculate Conception of the Blessed Virgin Mary. Four years later, Bernadette Soubiros, a young person of fourteen years old and her family is the most poorest in

Lourdes, France, declared that she saw a lady in the village dump. There, she and two other were gathering fire wood. After several visits, the lady asked Bernadette to return fifteenth more times, which she faithfully did. As a result, the whole world received a message and a great gift. The message was simple and direct:

"REPENTANCE, REPENTANCE, and REPENTANCE!"

The gift was a beautiful clear spring coming forth from the base of the rock at a point. This point was where Bernadette had obediently dug with her hands, hard in the mud. A lady requested and directed her to drink from the spring. Water soon displayed miraculous healing powers, and pilgrims began their journeys to Lourdes to bathe in the water and drink out of the spring.

Even since the spring appeared, countless pilgrims have found this living water as this spot where the Blessed Virgin spoke to a young person of no account. When Bernadette at last asked the beautiful lady who she was, the virgin confessed with awesome simplicity,

"I AM THE IMMACULATE CONCEPTION."

Free from sin from the beginning, she showed what the Lord wants of us at the end. Her battle is ours, a fight against sin, against the devil himself. If we could only repent our sins, the calamities that threaten the human race would never occur.

Like water from the rock, from it would be the healing and peace that come from the heart of GOD. Just like Holy Mary, we dwell within the old rock of the church, the rock of Christ. The water cleanses and freshens us with grace.

The miracles at Lourdes continue until today, to confront us with the message of Holy Mary and immediate abilities of God's healing and forgiveness.

That spring is a reminder to the people of the world that we must repent and drink the water of forgiveness. In turn, He will wash our stains away, if we repent and reconcile with GOD!

The message grew more emphatically with Lourdes that sins is the core of the problem. Obviously, the world must change as the darkness of sins is gathering.

Two years ago, I visited Lourdes in the South of France with my family. We all felt the peace flowing like a river from the spring of living water.

Change your holiday agenda, go there and experience it for yourself. It is not too late!

The Warning, the Miracle, the Punishment

The Blessed Virgin Mary promised that the sign which will appear after the miracle at Garabandal in Spain will be permanent. What a strong statement for us to swallow!

You may think now what sign, which Mary mentioned for whom and for what? It does not matter what we think or believe anymore, because the sign will appear as our Blessed Mary said so!

Little has it been revealed about the nature of this sign.

We know the following details; it will remain until the end of the world. We will be able to see, photograph and televise it, but not touch it. No one will be able to explain it. It will remind us forever of the great miracle. Anyone who wishes to see it will go to Garabandal and examine the sign. It will recall to our minds that God summons the world to repent, and testify throughout time that the Lord insist by its presence that the world will indeed end one day; That Jesus will come again on the "clouds of heaven" to make all things new, and to judge the living and the dead.

The sign will be there in the midst confronting us, crying out by its very presence, repentance! As did our lady in Lourdes, it will not let us forget that the punishment will surely come if the warning and the miracle are ignored.

The sign will focus our attention on the truth that God has clearly intervened, on this mountain just as He said on Mount Sinai, Mount Calvary, and Mount Caramel and at a Pentecost on Mount Zion to call his people to Himself.

At Garabandal, for the first time in history, the Lord himself will set his own sign as a perpetual memorial of his saving act for today's world.

The sign will point to heaven. It will tell us always that this present life will one day end, and that we will ascend, as Jesus and Mary did, to eternal life that is beyond the clouds and our understanding.

Our destiny is to live forever with God in heaven. The permanence of the sign will persuade us to keep our eyes fixed, not on earthly, but on heavenly things. Avoiding sin and embracing heaven's holy way does this.

The sign will recall to us that it was because of sin that the former world was destroyed and rejected. It will continue to alert us that sin wrecks lives and happiness. It will cast light on our sins and show to be the true enemy.

The period of peace that our Lady promised at Fatima will come. The sign will protect the era of peace by talking to each to be peace with his brothers and sisters, with self and with God. Peace is a give for the heart, and if heart is at peace, it can give away peace. Peace in me can make the world around me more peaceful place for others.

Peaceful nations are made of peaceful persons who have chosen peace as a way of life for themselves.

There can be no war between nations full of peaceful men and women. A heart transformed by one's own inner peace can give the world the peace that the world cannot give itself.

Those share, through repentance and conversion, the peace of Jesus, who will inaugurate the era of peace promised to us all.

People of peace can hasten it, delayed by people who reject peace and embrace sin. We only know that it will certainly come, this mysterious "peace." The immaculate heart has promised it.

God himself has begun, by the upcoming warning to dramatically make clear to us that what Mary has proclaimed has been true all along. We can all see for ourselves what God is doing, because He is making His work apparent.

No one can sincerely maintain it from now onwards that there is no God or that He has no power.

We are experiencing his judgment upon our world, which has drifted so far from Him. In His mercy, He now gives us the opportunity to turn back to Him before it's too late.

We must wait now for the warning and then within a year of the date of the miracle with its permanent sign. It will eventually convert the whole world.

There is an era of peace stretching our before us. We must reach out for it, grasp it, and give it to one another. We can not delay any longer, only God knows how much time we have left. The time is now!!

Concentrate on the Holy Spirit the centre of every church and religion. Follow Him, who is the Living God on earth amongst us able to unite us all with God to an everlasting peace and life.

The Story of the Rosary

I am not surprised at all when you say, "What Rosary story? " Unless you are a Catholic or one of the people healed by the power of Holy Rosary prayer, you will not understand. This is very sad indeed because Rosary is not for selected people.

The Rosary is one of the church's greatest treasures and over the years, since the Blessed Virgin Mary herself gave it to us in the early 12th centuries, it has proved itself to be one of the most forms of prayer in honor of our Blessed Lady. Every day throughout the world millions of people recite the Holy Rosary in obedience to the Blessed Virgin Mary. Remember:

Monday and Saturday

"The Joyful Mysteries" "The Annunciation" + "The Visitation"
"The Presentation" + "The Finding in the Temple"

Thursday

"Luminous Mysteries Thursday" + " Jesus Baptism in the Jordan" + " Jesus self-manifestations at the Wedding at Cana" + "Jesus proclamation Kingdom of God with the call to conversion" + "Transfiguration of Jesus" + "Institution of the Eucharist as the Sacramental expression of the Paschal Mystery" +

Tuesday and Friday

"The Agony in the Garden" + "The Sourging at the Pillar" + "The crowning with Thorns" + "The Varying of the cross" + "The crucifiction"

Sunday and Wednesday

"The Resurrection" + "The Ascension" + "The Descent of

the Holy Spirit" + "The Assumption" + "The Crowning of Mary"

It is a most effective means to stay in touch with God and to overcome the evils of modern society. Prayer can restore peace to the world and save our souls. Saints have acclaimed this effectiveness and Popes in all ages have recognized it as a rich source of divine blessing.

The Rosary oriented around the year of 1208, during the period when St. Dominic had preached for years to members of his church without much success. One night while praying in the chapel of Notre Dame in Prouille, Our Lady appeared to him, holding a Rosary on her hand. She then taught him how to pray the Rosary and bade him to teach it to the world, promising that it would convert sinners and obtain graces for the just.

St. Dominic won many souls back to his church through constant teaching and praying of the Rosary.

At that time it must have been hard to believe that Our Blessed Virgin Mary appeared to him and gave him the Rosary.

In the year 1627, when King Louis XIII moved against the rebellious Huguenots, he ordered the public to recite the Rosary prayers. As a result, victory was won and France was saved for the Catholic faith.

We have proven that in 1857 in Lourdes, France, the Blessed Virgin appeared 18 times to Bernadette Soubirous. Bernadette tells us what happened in her own way of the apparition:

"I saw a lady dressed in white. She wore a white dress and a white veil with a blue waist band and a yellow flower on each foot, and she held a Rosary in one arm. The lady took the Rosary and made the sign of the cross with it. I managed to do likewise. I got down on my knees and began to recite the Rosary with the beautiful lady. The apparition moved the Rosary beads between her fingers without moving he lips."

During the 18th apparitions on March 25, 1858, she announces to Bernadette, "I am the Immaculate Conception," and from that day on everyone had no choice as to believe.

The Road Home

A s a hotelier moving through nine countries in three continents, I have a little choice with my wife and two kids, to join one global family, different religions, nationalities, skin colors, foods and traditions.

In such a world, a genuine acceptance of different lifestyles is necessary. Sadly, I've observed that most people choose to selfishly build their own separate heaven.

I studied and learned to respect all religions during my journey through people in the real world. I am not a sociologist, anthropologist, an economist, a psychologist, neither a priest; I'm just an ordinary man, who is ready to open his mouth, heart and mind, to share the burning news with the people.

Until late afternoon on 24ᵗʰ June, 1981, Medugorje was unknown, God forsaken small village, lost on high plateau in the central region of Bosnia (Yugoslavia), a communist country that was ruled by strong man Marshal Tito.

That evening at about 6:00 PM., six village children near rocky hills had a vision. They later claimed under an oath that they saw a beautiful young woman with a child in her arms. She had a heavenly smile, but did not speak at that time.

The lady appeared for the next two days. On the third day, Vicka one of the children, sprinkled holy water towards apparitions and said, "If you are our lady, stay with us. If you are not, be gone." The lady smiled and stayed. Mirjana, another of the children, asked the lady's name, and the lady replied, "I am the Blessed Virgin Mary."

From that day on, the Blessed Virgin Mary appeared almost every day. Today, 16 years later, these children, now teenagers, still see our lady almost every night.

Millions of people (Catholics, non-Catholics, Atheist) visit Medugorje. Miraculous cures have taken place; and cases of conversion are innumerable. The local government reacted unfavorably towards these activities and even jailed the priest!

Some ecclesiastical authorities fought against it, but couldn't stop it. Teams after teams of scientists, doctors, bishops, and theologians have scientifically examined this phenomenon and all have come to a conclusion: "No human science can explain the events of Medugorje, which belongs to the area of supernatural."

Medugorje is spiritual reality, a revival of Lourdes and Fatima. God uses Mary's apparitions today to fulfill the same prophecy role of the prophets in the past to bring people back to God.

This is what Medugorje is all about, it helps you to pray, to reconcile with God and deepen the understanding of the spiritual values of life.

The fruits of Medugorje continue all over the world. People doing penance, practicing weekly fast, praying with their hearts, are growing spiritually in love and service towards others.

There is no running on tangents, no exaggerations, no undue emphasis on one point over another······ only simple appeal to come to God through faith, conversion, prayer, and fasting, in order to find God and peace which we alone cannot give.

Our lady speaks of peace with God and men. Peace is the ultimate goal of life. This true peace can be achieved only through faith, the fundamental condition to communicate with God, (through conversion that is the change of heart which really pleases to God at the centre of our lives), through continued prayers to foster a relationship of love with God and our fellow men.

Through fasting, we gain our self control, which alone makes man capable of giving himself to God through a deeper form of spirituality.

This Catholic doctrine is too often overlooked by people today. This is the essence of Medugorje message, "To lead souls back to God."

When I first heard about Medugorje in 1984, it took me five years to make the decision to go to Medugorje. I jumped into a plane on December 8, 1989, and flew for 10 days, from Hong Kong to Zurich, to Belgrade. Then I hoped into a bus to Mostar, and finally to Medugorje, a journey with an encounter with my inner self, harvesting an essential back to basic principle, like praying the daily rosary, fasting for self control, and to do penance.

I was privileged to attend the Christmas message given by our Blessed Virgin Mary on December 15, 1989 at 10:00 P.M, on the Mount Podrobo. This vision dialogue was attended by less than 100 pilgrims from around the world. Nuns, priests, civilians and few humble people like me.

Marija, one of the visionaries, had the dialogue on Croatian language with our Lady. The message was later translated into English, German, Italian and other languages.

The message was very clear and precise: "Tell all people to pray, fast, sacrifice (especially during Christmas and Lent), to grow in your spiritual life, and to come closer to God."

The essence of the message is to lead souls back to God.

Herewith I fulfill my promise given to the Blessed Virgin Mary on December 15, 1989, to spread the urgent message to all people, regardless of race, age or religion. God doesn't make the difference between peoples, we are the ones responsible for the difference that we create amongst ourselves. The devil with his smooth way to win our souls through pleasure, materialism, selfish is indeed a successful businessman. Look at what devil has done to the world!

Are you on the road home? Don't wait because you don't know how much time you have left.

God loves us so very much and he wants us to come home safely.

The People I Met on The Road Home

T hroughout my journey I've met such extraordinary people who have touched my heart and have over the years, become my own personal mentors in both my professional and private life.

*Yam Atallah is the President of the Chaine des Rotisseur in Paris managing the Bailliage for 85 Countries. With his firm Leadership ability, supported by his dedicated Board of Directors Team Marie Jones and Klaus Tritschler. The Bailliage was born in Paris in 1248- 1950 and in Korea 1977 by Hans Junger+Gretl and Team. Then

In 2002 Hans handed over the Bailliage on my Shoulder.

The Essence of the Bailliage to met 5 Times a Year in one of the Leading Hotels or Restaurant serving quality Food and Wines.

Based on Friendship and comradely selected Members the Chaines is based on.

Photo from the Chaine Inductions.

The Highlight in 2019 the Bailliage for the first time has been ask to host the first Global Young Sommelier Contest from 15 Countries in Sep 17-21th.

My favourite TV Show send by Deutsche Welle is Markus Lenz.He is able to collect the most unique People around the World sharing their Live experience. Nobody can escape his sharp focus Questions from the Markus is from Sued Tirol my favourite Part of Europe.

Helmut
Schmidt
___
Die Deutschen und
ihre Nachb rn

* I met Gerhard Schmidt and wife Loike at the Sheraton
Walker Hill and he signed his Book die Deutschen und die
Nachbar. After Adenauer he was my Mentor in the Politics.

*Chan Jun Park Asia Director of Asia Wine Trophy.
Lectured The scovery of Daejeon 2019.

Adolf Schmitt Trier Weingut. He created the yearly Wine Testing in Daejeon, a roh Model for all Wines Experts in the World

* Mother Mary appeared to selected children in Fatima, Portugal, Lourdes-France, Medjugorje, former Yugoslavia, Naju-Korea, and Garabandal- Spain. The combined message is simple, easy to understand but difficult to follow come closer to God.

* Jaeger's Father Joseph und Frieda Muckernhirn are always in our hearts. They took us into their home and provided shelter and food, while my father Edmund was still in Russia fighting against the Cold Winter. He came home in 1947. Jaeger Mutter Frieda gave birth to Rita, Bernhard, and Supply, Erika our closest family as our newborn.

* My Father asked me to make an effort to work for American Company to show our respect for the given Marshal Plan by President Roosevelt, for his heroic Act of humanity for my Fatherland.
I followed my Father's request to worked with the United-States with Intercontinental Hotels owned by Pan Am, with ITT Sheraton based in Boston, with Starwood Hotels based

in White Plane NY, and Hilton International.

* I'm also joined as an active Member of the US National Ski Patrol in Korea since 1999 led by Roh Melon+Stanley Lobtell, Wayne Clerk, Bob and Wendel Moon.

* My eldest daughter is married to Shane, an ex American Navy Hero, living in West Virgina with their 3 Children Lexes, Dagoda and Noah.

* My second daughter, Alexandra,graduated from the Embry Riddle Aeronautical University in Daytona Beach, Florida, as a Commercial Pilot. The FAA recognized Alexandra Melati Brender a Lady Pilot sets positive example for others to follow.

* Frieda and Max Stemmle im Obertal. Hansjoerg und Josephine, Karl Joseph und Sabine, Victoria taking over the kitchen from Papa very well. Roland Fuchs and Monika living first in Neuhof then moved to Hamburg.

Roland Fuchs influenced my professional Carer taking a 3 Years Cock Apprentice at Hotel Victoria in Freiburg like he did, becoming a chef. Roland & Monika, shaped my professional and private live.

They will always be a part of the Brender's family.

Roland passed away Feb 6th at 1pm in Hamburg.

I was privilege in spending 10 Minutes Speech at his Funeral in front of his Familie Monika and Friends.

→ Mother Mary in Medugorje connected me with Pfarrer Riesterer a Missionary born in Untertal and stationed in Muenchen. He was a devoted Mother Mary Missionary. He helped me to fine-tune my holy Medugorje's Experience with my professional life.

*Henry Holly retired Navy Corporal devoted his entire life to Billy Graham's Mission spreading the Gospel. He single handed organized giant Crusades in Asia, which brought People closer to God.

*Ulli Stielike has been the National Soccer Coach building a strong Foundation for the Soccer Team. He remains in heart and mind forever together with his wife Doris.

→ Live lecture by Dr. Edward de Bono, who inspired me for the last two decades with his Tools for Parallel Thinking.

White Hat*   What information do we have?

Red Hat*   How do you feel about each possible design.

Green Hat*   Alternatives and creative the possibilities.

Yellow Hat*   Find the benefits of the Alternatives.

Black Hat*   Managing the Thinking Process. Find the defects and problems.

Meeting Bernhard Vogel a trusted German Friend in Korea, a famous Lawyer and trusted business Men. He inspired my own daughter Alexandra to become a Commercial Pilot few Years ago. I am proud to be his Friend forever.

* An Economists turned Hotelier is Hans Olbertz who believes striking the right balance between business, sports and family is the key factor for success. Either on the Job, at the Squash + Tennis Court, + Ski + Golf Course Hans and Gabi have been in front of them all.

* Peter Jentes the first GM to open the Grand Hyatt in Seoul set a brilliant Standard until this present Days. A true example what Leadership is all about. Training and building countless Employees to take over the Hotel & Tourism Industry.

* Never to be forgotten my time at the Manila Intercontinental led by Dir of F&B Peter Stevens a role Model in our Industry. Together with the Kitchen Team led by Executive Chef Roland Fuchs,+Peter Stevens+Roger Begre+Werner Meier Josef Diener.
Top Restaurant Manager Dieter Becht and Michael Sergeda.

* Jay Hahn offered me a Job at the Sheraton Walker Hill in 1991 as Resident Manager. Then VIP. I stayed for 8 Years, coming from Hong Kong. He becomes my life Mentor because of his most passionate positive Attitude. My Family will always admire and love him forever.

* My dear colleague Chef & close Friend 「Franzle」 Wilfried Christen. Our time in Bali playing Tennis+Bowling and cooking will never be forgotten while his secretary was Tati Diasvera my wife since then. He was an Executive Chef

with Hyatt Hotels in Bali and Denpassar.

After lots of health challenges he let go and left us too soon March in December 2015.

* Swiss born Werner Meister a top Executive Chef with Hyatt Bangkok with Souschef's Wilfried Christen and Erwin Graf.

* Erwin Graf has been my a loyal Executive Chef at the Sheraton Walker Hill & Grand Hilton in Seoul for over 5 Years.

* Walter Kessler who welcomed me at the Airport in 1991 with my Familie arriving from HKK to the Sheraton Walker Hill. A very close friend since Intercontinental in Genf, London, Manila. He lost his Mother recently former Swiss Air Executive. She is in our Prayers,

* Hanspeter Schwanninger from Bangkok the Owner of his Restaurant the Hosentraeger.
He has been the Executive chef and GM at the Narai Hotel.
He passed away and left a lovely Familie behind.

* My Korean friend Chabum Soccer Star with Winni Sturm from the Faust Gymnasium Staufen in Germany. Winfried Stürm, Mint Lehrer Founder of 30 Jears Hardware AG.

* My Nephew Gerhard Daiger Owner of Dr. Walser Dental in Radolfzell.

A rising Star is Gerhard and his Team demonstrating innovative Products for the Dental field around the World.

He got the reward from Lothar Spaeth among the 100 best middle Company in Germany.

He got the Gold-jupiter Preis und zum Ehren Senator gekroennt.

Kuerzlich vom Justizministerium zum Handelsrichter im Ehrenamt erhoben.

* To my dear friend Berthold und Endan. They visit me in Korea after 30 Years. He is a role Model for young and old how to manage Knowledge and Time together in a foreign Land.

* Werner Berger and Otmar Frei in Manila for their generous effort bring "SEAC" together based on Comradely and friendship.

* To Henry Holly a disciple of Billy Graham showing me a safe way to Jesus Christ our savior.

*To Lee Kuan Yew Past President from Singapore who told me in 2002 at the Westin Chosun that "Believe in Yourself" nothing else will do. He turned Singapore into a Financial Hup single handed all recorded in his Red-binded book which he signed for me at the Westin Chosun in 2002.

Meeting Lee Kuan Yew I met in 2002 prime Minister from Singapore at the Westin Chosun. After singing his Book he said to me,

"Just believe in Yourself."

I met Mr. Schremp CEO from Mercedes＋Klaus Mangold＋ President＋Busch and Barbara.

By the way Gabi the wife of my brother Edmund in Munchen was selected to cut the hair of Barbara whilst they have been in Munich.

Klaus Mangold was wondering how can a naive Muenstertaeler von Obermuenstertal learning Koch can end as GM Position in Korea at the Westin Chosun. I told him my Curiocity and Ergeiz brought me here.

Bernhard Brender and Gerhard Daiger

Bernhard's Father, Edmund, Herbert, Margret, Fransis+

Morgenland Baldasar+Melchor Casbar arrive at the GHS. Jutta
Hassler the Catholic Parish with Mr. Hahn, und Sternsinger Baldasar+
Melchor+ Sebastian

Alexandra

The Brender's and Smiths
Alexandra, Bernhard, Taty
Luisa, Noah (in belly), Shane Lexess

Luisa, Bernhard's eldest daughter, and her family.
Luisa followed her father's footsteps and went into Hotel
Management, graduating top of her class at Ecole Hôtelière In
Lausanne.

She is now happily married to Shane, graduate of the American Navy. They have three beautiful children, Lexess Augustina, and Noah Michael.

In Lausanne!

Bernhard's grandson, Noah Michael

Bernhard's youngest daughter, Alexandra, taking her father out for a nice flight.

She graduated in Dec 14th 2009 Bachelor of Science in Aeronautical Science from Embry-Riddle Aeronautical University/Daytona Beach Florida.

Papa and Mama met through Philadelphia cheese cake at the Hyatt in Bali.

THE ROAD HOME

Youngest executive chef in Bali Intercontinental hotel.

Margret (family name) won the most Championship Record

***

*The Australian Open Singles 1960-71 1973

*Wimbledon Championships Single 1963+1965 1970

*United States Open Singles: 1962 1965,1968-70 1973

*French Open Singles: 1962+1964+1969-70 1973

*Italian Championship Singles 1962-64

*South African Open Singles; 1968+1971

*German Open Singles; 1964+ 1965+ 1966

*Federation Cup 1963-65 +1968-69+1971

Margret won every single match she played 20 out of 20

***

Finally the Mission of this book is to spread its urgent message to the People around the World to love one another, to repent, and to pray together. When People walk together we can make the world a better place.

Subject: The World's six best doctors

The World's six best doctors. worth reading twice

Steve jobs Died a billionaire at age 56. This is his final essay.

I reached the pinnacle of success in the business world. In some others' eyes, my life is the epitome of success. However, aside from work, I have little joy. In the end, my wealth is only a fact of life that I am accustomed to. At this moment, lying on my bed and recalling my life, I realize that all the recognition and wealth that I took so much pride in have paled and become meaningless in the face of my death.

You can employ someone to drive the car for you, make money for you but you cannot have someone bear your sickness for you. Material things lost can be found or replaced. But there is one thing that can never be found when it's lost- Life. Whichever stage in life you are in right now, with time, you will face the day when the curtain comes down.

Treasure love for your family, love for your spouse, and love for your friends. Treat yourself well and cherish others. As we grow older, and hopefully wiser, we realize that a $300 or a $30 watch both tell the same time. You will realize that your true inner happiness does not come from the material things of this world. Whether you fly first class or economy, if the plane goes down- you go down with it.

Therefore, I hope you realize, when you have mates, buddies and old friends, brothers and sisters, who you chat with, laugh with, talk with, have sing songs with, talk about north-south-east-west or heaven and earth that is true happiness! Don't educate your children to be rich. Educate them to be happy. So when they grow up they will know the value of things and not the price. Eat your food as your medicine; otherwise you have to eat medicine as your food.

The one who loves you will never leave you for another because, even if there are 100 reasons to give up, he or she will find a reason to hold on. There is a big difference between a human being and being human. Only a few really understand it. You are loved when you are born. You will be loved when you die. In between, you have to manage!

The six best doctors in the world are sunlight, rest, exercise, diet, self-confidence and **friends.** Maintain them in all stages and enjoy a healthy life.

The Grand Hilton my home since 2006 under Owner Chairmen Dong Won Lee, Son President Benedict and Andrew Kim, providing me the full Support to manage the Hotel together.

This booklet will soon be available in German and Korean Languages:

When People pray together and walk together we can make the world a better place.

Respectfully from the Author Bernhard+Tati in Korea+ Luise. Alex in USA,

Shall love, joy, peace, patience, kindness, goodness, faithfulness, self control guide you in good and challenging times.

To all the people who have touched our lives especially Theresa Gross sharing her wish to support The Mother Theresa Charity Fund.

To get a copy, send your request to:

e-mail: bernhard.brender@gmail.com
e-mail: Tatybrender56@gmail.com

Request a copy of the book for only US$ 19.50

Send the Money to the
Bernhard Brender+Standard Chartered Bank+Account number
130 20 388753 Swift Code scblkrse 0409160 9 jungga-ro Seodaemun-gu Seoul.

For your info I started a Charity Foundation in Kalcutta by the wish of Theresa Gross. Be part of Mother Teresa's Word's she said :
"Yesterday is gone, Tomorrow not yet come. Let's begin today."

Thank You!~ Dankeschoen~ Terimakasi Banjak~ Kamsahamnida.
Respectfully from the Author Bernhard+Tati in Korea+ Luise+Alex and Theresa in USA.

Additional 3 Messages for the Book the Road Home

▌ First Message today;

- It is my great Pleasure former Paradise vice Chairman Mr. Rak Jin Chung to include into my Book because he sponsored it generously.

- His talented Son Kyung Min Chung Ass. Director of General Affairs Paradise Group is the rising Star in the Company

- Shall the Lord bless the entire Catholic Family this 2019 Christmas and beyond

▌ Second Message today

KOREA CULINARY FAVORITES FOR LIFE

- Being in Korea since 1991 with my Family the most favorite Winter Fruit is Persimmon and fermented Kim chi

- Related to Korean Culture they have to respect the first

born especially if it is a Girl. She has to be respected equal as a boy, as long they are healthy and obey their Parents.

▌Third Message today.

KOREAN-GERMAN CULINARY LOVE AFFAIR

Hansik Korean Kitchen in Germany by Gernot Mueller and Kim Sung Suk and talented Son.

They open in Hofsteigstrasse 122A in 6971 Hard/Bodensee a OKIMS restaurant serving

MAKGEOLLI, SOJU, MANDU, DDUKBAEGI BULGOGI, AND MUCH MORE. Bringing such healthy Food to Germany is a smart move towards Happiness bringing both countries together.

For Koreans staying in Korea, or visiting Germany or Germans Citizens should take Advantage to taste "OKIMS" Korean delights. Reserve under 05574 73630.

이 도서의 국립중앙도서관 출판예정도서목록(CIP)은 서지정보유통지원시스템
홈페이지(http://seoji.nl.go.kr)와 국가자료종합목록 구축시스템(http://kolis-
net.nl.go.kr)에서 이용하실 수 있습니다.
(CIP제어번호 : CIP2019050996)

THE ROAD HOME

Author / Bernhard Brender
Publisher / Yeongran, Kim
Publication / Hannury Media
Editing Design / Seon-sook Ji

2F 40, Gurojoongangro18gil Gurogu Seoul, 08303
Telephone / 02) 379-4514, 379-4519
Fax / 02) 379-4516
E-mail / hannury2003@hanmail.net

Report Number / 25100-2016-000025
Report Date / 2016. 4. 11
Date of Registration / 1993. 11. 4

The First Publication / 2019. 12. 16

ⓒ 2019 Bernhard Brender Printed in KOREA

US $ 10.00

*The damaged books are exchangeable.
*It stamps are omilted through agreement with the author.

ISBN 978-89-7969-811-4 03850